By the Ri

Designed and typeset by Ray Wilkinson
Printed in Great Britain by Amazon

Back cover image by Pearson Scott Foresman
Title page images derived from original image by Pearson Scott Foresman

By the River

Clare Lehovsky

Dedicated to Grandma Anne Seidelin

List of Characters

She-Wolf:	The wolf who suckled Romulus and Remus, mythical founders of Rome. She sees the world through wolfish eyes, and gives names for different characters as outlined below:
Not-Man:	Mars, god of war, father of Romulus and Remus
Sun:	Romulus
Moon:	Remus
Oak-Man:	Numitor, grandfather of Romulus and Remus, king of Alba Longa
The Man:	Amulius, brother to Numitor and his usurper, responsible for ordering the deaths of Romulus and Remus
River:	The god of the River Tiber, or Tiberinus, as well as his daughters the naiads or river nymphs
Other-Man:	Fastulus, shepherd of King Amulius, who finds Romulus and Remus being suckled by She-Wolf and raises them as his own
Long-Fur:	Acca Larentia, wife of Fastulus, foster mother of Romulus and Remus
Sun and Moon's Dam:	Rhea Silvia, mother of Romulus and Remus. Her fate is contested
Not-Wolves:	Dogs

My Name is She-Wolf

My Name is She-Wolf.
I can Swim like the Fish in the Stream
I can Pounce like the Wildcat
Tremble like a Mouse
Hear like an Owl
I Know every Tree in the Glade, their Souls
Lead me Down to the River
The River is my Domain
For I am the Lone She-Wolf.
The River flashes Gold in Summer
And Smooth Silver in Winter,
It is a Gateway to All Other Worlds.
I am She-Wolf of the Forest.
I will Tell You What Happened
By the River.

Not-Man, Cubs and Revenge

He is a Man but not a Man.
Red courses through Men's veins.
Gold flows from Not-Man's wound,
A silver snail's shell is on his head.
"I am Mars," He said, staunching the golden flow.
He is carrying a Wolf-Biter too, like Man.
Not-Man's blood tastes of Light.
Light that sizzles on my teeth and tongue.
I look at him, He looks at me
Not at all like my Mate had been
"Why are you all alone?" He asks
He knows, he is taunting me
I will not rise to his bait.
"You will be of some use to me, Lupa."
I growl at him. That is not my name.

My name is She-Wolf. Like the others.
"I do not believe you are against making deals,
She-Wolf."
Not-Man says, taking his shell off,
His fur is like the colour of Dried Blood,
His scent not much different.
"If you leave this place, you will be forever Alone,
But if you stay, you will have two things:
Cubs and Revenge."
His snail-like body glints in the Light
He disappears into the wind, smiling.
He knows He has my Attention.

The Circle of Branches

From my Vantage Point I see River breathing.
He takes a small circle of branches
And places it onto the bank
I wait until Light darkens, then crawl to the bank.
Something is reflecting there.
The circle of branches has two white Orbs in.
Their noses are squashed against their Orbs,
Their paws are small and weedy.
No fur covers their pale bodies, instead
Something like dead skin covers them
I jump back and snarl,
Whining comes from the branches.
I come forward again to their wide orbs
And lick them with my tongue
It's not unlike the smooth underside of a paw.

Their whines turn into watery gurgles,
The Cave will give us shelter,
No one will find us there.
I know, for certain, they are not Wolves,
Nor other creatures of the forest.
They are Men – why do I keep them?
Men are the reason I am alone.
But Men must be the reason they are alone,
For River did not place them in the circle,
The circle that was cast into the water.
I grab the Branches in my Teeth
And drag them towards The Cave.
It is in a good position, not too far From the River.
It has a tree with gnarled roots
And dark fruit that hangs heavy
The Cave itself is large and flat
I can smell that Man is long gone,
There are Bones that could be his.
I prowl around the Orbs, still screaming now,
The sound flattens my ears
I nudge the circle of branches until it breaks,
The orbs tumble onto the cold leafy stone floor.
I lie down with a humph, my wound twinges
I ignore it and nudge their Orbs to my teats
Teats still bearing the bites of my cubs.

The Warning

The next day they are the same,
Same whines, same Rain falling down from their eyes.
I shall have to give them Names,
That might quieten them.
I know they are male,
And their faces are like the Sun and Moon,
One Orb has a little war-wound above his eye
Shaped like a Half-Moon,
That will do. He is Moon.
The other Orb is larger, seems brighter. He is Sun.
I go down to the River to drink.
Not-Man shimmers next to me while
I lap the cold water of River.
The same smell of Blood, the same snail-shell.
"Is it strange to you that you are licking River?" He asks

jovially,
Face creasing in entertainment.
Not-Man crouches down to the water,
Cupping one paw, he drinks with me.
Once we are sated, he rises up again. I back away.
"You have done well thus far, She-Wolf."
He says, staring deeply into my eyes,
His orb is shifting constantly.
"I stand by my promise that you will have
Cubs and Revenge.
But I give you a warning, this does not come lightly.
I know you want The Man."
My hackles rise and I growl. Not-Man breathes in anticipation of war.
"Yes. But this will come in time.
These Cubs you now have, they also desire Revenge."
I do not respond. I wait for him.
Not-Man looks out onto River before he speaks.
"These Cubs, your Cubs, they will have their
Revenge. Do you understand me?
Not until they have their Revenge you can have yours."
I will have to wait, wait until
These Cubs are grown.
Not-Man nods his Orb, satisfied.
"Do not kill The Man. Not yet.
His time will come."
His form shimmers, leaving me alone
Listening to the sound of My Cubs.

Oak-Man

The Old-Man is like a fallen Oak Tree.
He is sitting there on a stone as if struck.
If he had been a tree, cubs would have played
On his long branches.
His name is Oak-Man.
His Orb is tired, wrinkled like bark,
His skin smooth like leaves,
Oak-Man is looking out onto River.
Rain is not yet falling down his face,
Like that of the Cubs,
He is covered in one big skin
That smells of plants.
He is Old, yet he reminds me of
The aged Alphas one sometimes sees,
Who have not been challenged by a younger, Reckless Wolf

Although they are Old, they can Kill
With One Strike.
Instead, Oak-Man looks at River,
Making silent sounds to himself.
Sun and Moon are in his Orb,
They are in his Orb as much as he is in theirs.
I wonder if he knows of them
And if he would take them away from me.
So I wait, watch, until his eyes close
And his Orb relaxes into the rest of his body
The dimming sunlight reflects from the water
Onto his peaceful Orb.

The Man

I can hear Him through the forest. The Man.
His smell radiates off him,
Like some pompous stag about to challenge its rival.
"What say you, Amulius? Where next?"
The Man sniffs the air. I bare my teeth in a silent snarl.
"We keep going."
I freeze. I feel helpless,
like a rabbit started from the bushes by a fox.
Helpless as the hunting Not-Wolves Smell my Scent.
Sun and Moon are here. I need to protect them,
Protect them from Men.
Even if it means hiding.
"Wolf!"
I am discovered –
I jump over fallen trees and dart

Beneath hanging bushes.
My breath comes in ragged gasps,
A Not-Wolf latches onto my shoulder and hangs on.
"Good boy!" The Man says.
He calls the other Not-Wolf to his side
They are smaller than me but stronger.
"I know you." The Man says.
My eyes know him.
He levels his wooden stick at my heart.
Like he did with my Mate and Cubs.
I toss the Not-Wolf aside and launch Myself at him.
Blood pours out over my Fangs as he
Bellows like a Wounded Bull
Not-Man's warning
Is the only thing that stops me.
I use Man's body to twist myself away,
My Old Wound burning
A different path Takes me back
To the River
And my new charges I have
Protected.

Swimming Lesson

I enjoy the Light's Warmth
While I wait for Sun and Moon.
They topple out of the cave uncertainly
And head towards me, the only certainty.
Moon uses me to lift himself
His tiny paws bite into my side,
I growl to warn him.
Sun is moving on his own now,
He props himself up with a boulder
By the side of the Cave and looks around.
With Moon still hanging onto me,
I make my way towards the River.
The birds are waking up,
The trees are talking to one another,
Their forms floating in the breeze,

No Men to be seen here.
Sun follows his brother,
Copying me,
Sniffing when I sniff,
Falling back on his four paws
To scratch the ground when I did.
I snarl at him when he tugs my tail,
I am not a Not-Wolf.
This is A Chance for me to teach Them
How to swim like Wolves do.
Like I did my cubs. The ones that are no more.
River's daughters are here, too,
They will laugh at my attempts
To teach these Cubs
What should have been taught them
A long time Ago.

Other Man and Long Fur

A Rodent appears
Out of the thorny bush next to me,
I give chase and Almost have it
In my Grasp when I hear voices.
I whip my head around –
"What do we have here?"
A weathered voice speaks Out.
I can no longer hear the trees
Or the birds,
As Men walk by the River.
I am about to charge out of the bushes
When I realise it is not Him. Man.
But it must be – Man's voice.
But the voice is different, the smell, different.
Not-Man speaks behind me.

"Hold."
I Bare my Fangs silently.
Not-Man repeats again.
"Hold."
"Fastulus – I do believe they're babies!"
A softer voice speaks now, excited.
A mother anticipant of care.
I move away from Not-Man to look,
Another She-Man is crouching,
Extending her paw towards Sun.
Sun snaps at her with his little teeth,
He makes me a proud Wolf-Mother.
She withdraws her paw, surprised.
Her light long fur falls around her shoulders.
Her name shall be Long-Fur.
I have not encountered fur the colour
Of wheat before.
"He's like a dog!"
Other-Man grasps the top of his pointed stick
And looks around the forest.
"It could be, or it could be Wolves raising them."
"Wolves?" She cries,
Now scooping up Moon.
She thinks I am dangerous,
That I shouldn't have Sun and Moon
The babes I saved
They are Mine.
I can't Take It any longer.
I ignore Not-Man's warnings
And come into the open,
Just as Other-Man is about to pick up Sun.
We meet Face to Face.
I do not want Them to take Them

Just as Man had taken my Cubs.
I was not going to give them up
That easily Like Before
When they had snatched Them
While my Mate was lying dead
On the ground.

All Part of the Plan

When I make my presence known,
They see that I am there.
Other-Man stares straight back into my eyes,
Even when Long-Fur gasps fear.
His eyes are as blue as the sky above him.
Other-Man moves Sun towards Me
He knows that he shouldn't be afraid of me,
For we are Kindred Spirits,
And moves him gently to my Snout.
I sniff Sun's head
Before licking it, just once.
I would have liked to have licked
Moon, too, but Long-Fur is too Afraid.
She reminds me of me with Cubs.
She is now their Mother

A Mother of Wolves
We are always Afraid.
Afraid of dangers that Men
Do not See
She is afraid of my Amber eyes
Warning Her.
She shrinks back as Other-Man
Bows to me, then retreats backwards,
Still holding Sun.
Sun is confused, grasping at me,
Away from Other-Man
He does not know his own Kind.
Moon simply looks at me,
We have our farewell.
The new parents finally make their way back to where they
Came,
To where Men live,
Much Further Down the River.
I whip back round to Not-Man,
But he is no longer There.
I Edge out the Bushes,
Still waiting.
He Shimmers in front of me,
Just as I am going into
The Empty Cave.
I growl at him.
He has ruined everything.
"This is all part of the plan, She-Wolf,
You could not have raised them Forever."
But Not-Man had said that if
I stayed,
I would have Cubs and Revenge.
I have nothing,

Except an Empty Cave.
Not-Man fades into the air,
And the trees cautiously come back out
Of their bark shells,
And the trees start chirping again,
River and his Daughters watch me
From the Water.
I ignore them and retreat
Into the Cave, where all I have
Are Rat's bones for company.

The Branch Cave

I creep towards the Branch Cave
Where they are living now.
By the River.
Amongst their own kind,
The Wolf-killers.
Long-Fur is there. She is hanging
Up little bits of Animal Skin, on a long plant
Stretched across two flourishing Trees
Around the back of her Territory.
I see Sheep in Branch Squares.
Their Smell is So Tempting.
But I Must Watch Sun and Moon.
Sun is out there with her.
He is holding onto her leg, Whining.
He is sitting next to Long-Fur's

Circle of Branches.
Rain is running down his orb.
He is missing me.
I look around for Moon,
He is inside their Branch Cave,
He is Scraping across the floor.
Long-Fur finishes what she is doing
And Scoops Sun Up, placing him
In her Circle of Branches.
She carries him around Fast,
And he makes a strange sound
That I never heard him make
When he was with me.
It is like a Babbling Brook,
Gurgling and rising in frequency.
She goes back into the Branch Cave.
I can hear her make another noise too,
Not like speaking,
She is using her voice differently
It feels like the Wind in the Dark
After a while I can no longer hear
Either Sun or Moon.
I must go, for there are other
Branch Caves nearby,
Where Men might
See Me.

Wolf Paw Marks

I want to Growl Loudly at the sight of
Other-Man teaching Sun and Moon
How to Hunt.
How can He?
He has no Idea What he is Doing.
Sun strides behind Other-Man.
He is brandishing a small pointy stick,
Like the one Other-Man carries.
Moon trails behind his brother,
He is playing with several pieces of grass
In his paws, methodically and carefully
I know he Wishes to be
Inside the Branch Cave with Long-Fur.
Other-Man is now crouching by the River,
Touching the soil with his large paws.

"There. And there. Look, do you see, Rom?"
Sun squats down next to Other-Man,
Who he thinks is his Sire.
"Paws, they're paws, father!"
He twists round to Moon, quivering.
"Look Rem, paws!"
Moon sidles over and looks.
"Whose do you think it is?"
Other-Man asks.
"Animal." Moon mutters.
"We know that." Other-Man says,
"But what type?"
"Dog?" Sun asks, looking around
For Other-Man's Not-Wolves.
I wonder if Other-Man knew not
To bring them today.
I was watching from the shadows of my Cave,
Just by the Fruit-tree.
It is foolish of me to leave Marks,
But... if... They were to follow...
"Close enough. These are Wolf Paw Marks."
"Wolf?" Sun jumps back.
He clutches his pointy stick in his paw.
He Howls into the Quietness
Of the River.
I laugh quietly at his Attempt
Of being a Wolf
Now that he is no longer
With me.
He does not know
His true Heritage.

Other-Man Tells About Me

Moon snorts while Other-Man shushes Sun.
"That's enough, Rom.
Yes, you're Right, a Wolf has been Here.
She's watching us Right Now,
Her Den is Right Behind You."
The Cubs jump, and rightly so.
What is Other-Man doing,
Bringing Them Here?
Not-Man had made it clear
They would live with Other-Man.
"I bring you here because
You have the right to Know."
They look at Him.
"I am Not your Father,
And your Mother is not your Mother."

He says it with a sound that
An Old Dog might make
When sitting Down.
Sun and Moon open their mouths wide.
So wide that their mouths stretch
Across their orbs.
"What, father?" Sun stammers.
"I found you, Here. On this Bank.
This River."
Other-Man gestures to the water
Running beside them.
"There was a Wolf. I did not see her
At first.
I only saw You. Your mother and I
Had been Praying for sons.
This felt like a Miracle."
He corrects himself.
"Was a Miracle. It was a Miracle,
Sent by the Gods. You found Us more
Than we found You."
Other-Man watches my cubs intently.
Moon is looking towards the Cave
As if he is remembering something.
"I...remember a lot of Fur..."
Sun shakes his head at his Brother.

Sun Sees Me

He turns to Other-Man, drops his stick.
"This isn't true. You're my Father.
Who would do this to us, feed us to
The Wolves?"
And ignoring Other-Man's calls,
Runs straight into the bushes
Towards Me.
He stops.
Stops like a Wolf struck dead By a Stick.
He sees my eyes gazing
Back at him in the bushes.
I do not say anything.
For what could he understand?
I cannot do anything – Not-Man.
I simply stand there in the bushes

And watch my Cub Retreat.
In fear of Me.
He runs straight back to Other-Man.
Other-Man sees his orb and calls Moon.
"Rem, time to go."
"But..." Moon gestures to my Cave.
He is floundering like a beached Minnow,
Tossed from the water
Onto the rocks to breathe Air.
Other-Man looks at him, one paw
On Sun's shoulder. He is looking
Into the undergrowth around
Where I am.
"I know I am not your Father.
But it is my duty to look after you,
Still.
The Gods entrusted You to Us.
So we will Continue.
Your Mother is waiting.
Do you want to hurt Her?"
Long-Fur. Not their Real Mother.
Moon mumbles and shakes his head.
Sun stiffens under Other-Man's paw.
"Let's go." Other-Man says finally.
He guides Sun and a floundering Moon
Back towards their
Home of Men.

They Both See Me

Sun creeps towards Me through the leaves,
I see Rain dripping off his Orb.
He is a Little Older from when he last saw
Me.
Moon tugs at Sun's white skin that flaps around
His legs.
"No, don't, Rom, Father said..."
Sun ignores Moon and reaches out his paw.
I look into his Eyes and
See that I am Not in Them.
All I see Reflected in his Eyes is a Wolf.
A Hunter seeking Prey.
At this, I flatten my ears and snarl.
Sun jumps back with a yelp
And snatches his Paw away from

My Snapping Teeth.
He whirls around and runs.
Moon is already ahead of him –
They both would have had tails
Between their legs if they'd had any.
Their Howls soon Vanish into the Leaves.

Growing Up

I do not like watching Sun and Moon Become Men.
They are not like Other-Man,
Although they tend his Sheep,
Sheep that we Wolves Covet.
While I like to take Some
That have Strayed Near the River,
I would not go near The Branch Caves.
I have Grown, Too.
I would Rather have Lived in a Den
With my Mate and Cubs, Our own little Pack.
Watching them Grow,
Birthing new Cubs,
Letting the Pack flourish.
Yet, Now, all I do Is watch Sun and Moon
Hunt what is Mine,

They take their Kills
To She-Man, who prepares
The food that They eat.
They also attack Men,
Which is what I like To See.
They have not Entirely
Forgotten my Teachings.
If there are Men
Wandering in their Territory,
Moon distracts them,
While Sun and their Pack
Of Young-Men come
Down the Banks and Attack
Taking Shiny Things
They divide Amongst Themselves.
They play like Young-Wolves do.
I Hear, each Time,
Their Howls Echoing off the Trees
Now, I cannot count how Many
Young-Men are roaming
The Hills near The River.
I listen to the Trees Talking about the Young-Men,
River's Daughters Are Scared of Them
That is how I know
They could be Wolves, If not in Flesh.

The Large Gathering

It is that Time of Year When,
After the Winter is Thawing
Other-Man and other Men
Evoke an Anti-Wolf Not-Man
To protect their Sheep from Us.
The River is Cold,
Beginning to return
To its Summer Warmth.
I hear the Whoops of
Sun and Moon's Young-Men
As they prepare
For their Large Gathering.
I am in my Cave,
Wondering what I am Doing Here.
I should be Far Away By Now,

Looking for a Mate.
And start a new Pack.
It is Too Long
To be Lonely.
Not-Man has not Come
All Winter.
I wonder what he has been up to.
The Trees and River's Daughters
Are making my Hackles rise.
Their inane conversation annoys me.
I hear Footsteps
And Smell Sun
And Other-Man
They are Talking Loudly
By the River.
I edge Closer to Listen.
"Father, they have taken Rem,
What are we doing Here? By Now
The robbers will have taken him to
The King."
Other-Man Interrupts.
His voice is Urgent.
"Romulus, you must Listen.
You Remember When I brought you
Here, so many Years ago?
"Yes." Sun said.
"The She-Wolf."
His Voice is Tight.

Other-Man's Mind-Thoughts

"I have been Thinking."
Other-Man says,
"Around the time we Found you,
The King had ordered two
Babies to be Exposed."
Sun sucks in Breath.
"You Think We
Are Royalty?"
"I am from the Royal Household"
Other-Man says,
"I now Remember Rhea Silvia, daughter of
Numitor,
Was imprisoned by Amulius
For becoming Pregnant
By Mars

While she was a Vestal.
Amulius wanted to Destroy
His Brother Numitor's Males.
Amulius had the Babes
Committed to the River.
He wanted them to die."
Man. Man was the Reason
That Sun and Moon
Had been Alone.
I growled ever so softly
This is why Not-Man
Wanted Me Here.
Sun, Moon and I
Had the Same Man
To Kill.
I do not know if Other-Man
And Sun heard my Growl.
"Come, we should Go,
Before it is Too Late."
Other-Man says.
Sun agrees, and Their Footsteps
Return along the River
To their Branch Caves.

I Understand

I Understand
Sun's Feelings,
What he must be Feeling.
I know What it is Like,
For Man to take away
Your Position in Life,
I was Alpha-Female,
My Mate Alpha-Male.
Man killed my Alpha-Mate,
Now my Eldest Cub
Reigns in My Place
With Her Alpha-Male.
My Young-Cubs,
I Took with Me,
Despite the Pack,

Then Man Took Them,
Too,
They are Gone.
The Mind-stories
Are Back Now.
My Mate on the Grass
Dried Blood at his Throat
From Man's Not-Wolves
My Cubs, Their Little Bodies
Slung Over His Shoulder
His Shoulder I want to Bite
My Shoulder, Bleeding
Taking my Strength
Away.
Man will feel
My Breath on His Neck
Not Before Too Long.
I Shall Take
My Revenge.
The Man Bones from the Cave
Come back in my Vision,
Man will be like that
Soon.

A Sign From Not-Man?

I wait for a sign from Not-Man,
So my Revenge Will not be Taken
Away From Me.
We Wolves are not like Not-Wolves
Pouncing at a Chance.
A Woodpecker attacks the trees,
It's a hollow sound, frequent
Echoing off the other trees
By the River.
He is greener than the Leaves
Around Him.
As I watch, He flies Away,
Leaving Behind
The smell of Dried Blood.

Is that Not-Man giving me
A Sign
That my Time has Come?

I Leave the River

I Leave the River,
I bound Away from the Cave
That has Kept me Here
For so Many Years.
Years that could have been
Filled for Me.
Filled with life, love,
Not two Man-Cubs
Snatched away from me.
My Purpose in Life
May not have been
To have more Cubs
But there is certainly Revenge
Not-Man has promised That.
He may have let me have more Cubs

Only for a Short Time,
But Revenge I Shall Have Forever.
River and His Daughters know I am Going.
They rise their flowing heads
As a Farewell
The Trees shrink inside their Bark
They are Afraid.
I raise my head and see the Land,
The Hills, the River, the Forest,
A Breeze, then a Violent Wind
Causes the River Folk to sink
Beneath the Water,
The Trees to Sway,
While I HOWL.
I can help Sun
In the Way of the Wolves,
So that Moon is Saved
And Man Killed.
I do not know if I will Survive This.
This is, as Not-Man said, my Destiny.
But, for Now, I am,
And will always be
SHE-WOLF.
She-Wolf of the Forest,
She-Wolf of the River,
Now
She-Wolf of the Running Bank
As She-Wolf Runs
Runs towards
The World of Men.

Sun Hunts Like a Wolf

I am pleased to see that Sun
Hunts like a Wolf.
Not All in One Go, like Men,
Dim-wittedly,
As if they are completely asking for Death,
He sends in his Young Men
At Different Times,
Like Wolves do
So the Prey is surrounded
Without Knowing it
Before they leap on
And rip the life out of
Their Throats.
He knows that he has not
Enough Men

For Open Attack.
That is why he does This.
This pleases Me,
For I am able to
Watch and Observe
The Young Men
Act Like Wolves
Focusing in on
The Prey
Who do not Know
They are Coming
While they are celebrating
The Anti-Wolf Not-Man,
The Lupercalia,
A Rite long to be established
Long after we are gone
It doesn't even work anyway,
For I am Amongst Them.
They have no Idea who they are
Dealing with
She-Wolf of the Forest.
Who lived by the River
Alone, Raising their Kind
Who knows them as well as
They know Themselves,
That is the Power I have over them
That gives me strength
To begin this Attack.

I Flit Between the Shadows

I Feel like I am Flitting
Between the Shadows
They are Bending Themselves
To Me.
Is Not-Man
The Reason for this?
For I cannot do this Alone
I am not that kind of Power.
The Men do not See Me,
The Not-Wolves do not
Smell me.
I see that Oak-Man
Has Diverted Man's Men
Pretending there is
An Attack,

He is Wise
The Oak-Tree would be proud
Of his namesake being as Wise
As he Is.
I see Moon padding Along
With more Young-Men
To join his Brother
Oak-Man Must have
Seen Him
And realised he is His
They advance on Man
And Back him into
A Corner.
As was forewarned by Sun
Or am I seeing it played over Again?
Has my little half-moon already been
Captured,
My old Eyes and Mind deceiving me.
Moon was not built for Battle
As Sun was.
I follow Behind Them
Using the Shadows.

Revenge

Man's face is still Scarred
From My Attack.
"Who are you?" He Snarls
At Sun, Moon next to him.
"Don't you Remember Us,
Great-Uncle?"
Sun Asks.
Man's face turns from Red
To Pale.
"You...you were Drowned"
He Says.
His Eyes flick Between Them.
"That was Your Mistake."
Moon Says.
"Where is Our Mother?"

Sun Asks.
He is carrying a Wolf-Biter,
Like Man Before Him.
Man opens his Mouth,
But stops, Seeing Me
Behind Sun and Moon.
"You..."
I pad between Sun
And Moon
They suck in Breath
As my Fur Brushes
Past Them.
"Mother Wolf,
What are You
Doing Here?"
Moon says.
They know me.
At Last.
"Your... Mother..."
Man twists his Orb
"Of course. She has
Come
For
Revenge."
He shakes his Orb.
"For Who,
It Does Not Matter."
I growl. He knows exactly
How to get to me.

His Mistake

"I Ask you"
Sun edges Forward
"Tell us Where
Our Mother Is."
"This One, or
Your Real Mother?"
Man taunts like
A Desperate Beta Wolf.
"I will Never tell You
Where She Is
The Secret Stays with
Me... and You."
He launches Towards
Sun
Ignoring Me,

His Mistake.
I Leap Up
And Grab Him
By the Throat
Like how Not-Wolves Do
Sun Reaches
With his
Wolf-Biter
And Strikes Him
Until Blood Pours
Down my Whole Body.
I Do Not Care
We Wolves love Blood
Especially Man's.
The Wolf-Killer.
My Mate and Cubs
Are Avenged
Sun and Moon
Are Avenged.
Man's body falls to the Ground
Taking Me With Him.

Sun and Moon's Dam

I Do Not Even Have
A Name
For Sun and Moon's
Dam
I will call her
Sun and Moon's Dam
For she Reminds Me
Of Me.
The name That
Moon called Me
Must Mean the Same
Sun pushes Man
Off Me
And says
"Mother Wolf,

You Saved Me."
I breathe Shallow
I smell Dried Blood
Man's Wolf-Biter
Pierces Me
Through my
Old Wound.
Not-Man is There
Disguised as
Oak-Man's Helper
Bringing Oak-Man
To Them
Supporting Sun and Moon's
Dam,
Who has Sun and Moon
In her Orb.
"Romulus..."
Oak-Man speaks
And
The two Men
Turn Around
For that is
What They Are
Now.
My work here is Done.

Here Is Your Mother

"Here is Your Mother,
She was in the Prison
All this Time."
"Amulius lied."
Moon says to Sun.
Oak-Man leads Their
Mother to Them
She is as Pale
As River's Daughters
And as Fragile
As a Leaf
That could be Blown
Away by a Strong Wind.
She Stares down at Me
And we Know

Each Other
I am Her
She is Me.
"Sun, She's Going..."
Moon says.
They do not Notice
Not-Man leaving
Oak-Man
And coming To
My Side.
He stretches his Orb
At Me
Into a Wolf's Grin.
He holds Out a Paw
And my Soul
– for that is What
We Wolves Call Them too,
Follows Him.

New Territory

Oak-Man is Alpha,
And it is Time
For Sun and Moon
To Mark Out
Their Own Territory.
They Want to Make
Territory Near where
They Grew Up
By the River.
They do Man Things
Like look to the Skies
At birds,
I Stand Next to Not-Man
As we Observe.
"This is how They will

Do it,
In the Future"
Not-Man says
He is sensing my
Disdain.
I Hear Raised Voices
And see Sun and Moon's
Men Fighting
Each Other,
I Tense as I See
Sun and Moon
Acting like
Reckless Young Male Wolves.
Moon leaps over
Sun's new Markings
And Sun, before
My Eyes,
Pierces His Brother
In the Chest
With his Wolf-Biter.

His Brother's Blood

The Young-Men do not See Me
As I Make Straight
For Sun
As he Brandishes
His Wolf-Biter,
Over Moon,
Howling
"So Perish whoever
Leaps over my Walls!"
Moon is on the Ground
Like My Mate
Like My Cubs
Fresh Blood on his
Chest
I Flicker in Anger

And only Sun
Hears my Growl.
No-one Else
Sees Us
See Each Other.
He Knows I
Saved Him
And he Killed my Cub
In Return.
I look at Him
And He Looks at Me,
His Brother's Blood still
Mingling with the Earth.
At that Moment
His Eyes Show Fear
As he Realises Who I Am
And Who He is
"You're Dead..."
He says
"We burned You."
His eyes move to
Not-Man
Watching from
A Distance
He exhales Breath
"Mars?"

I Leave Sun

I Snarl and Bare My
Teeth
Making Him Look
At Me
My Eyes Say
I Cannot Forgive Him
For what He Did
I am Leaving Him
He Realises This
"Mother Wolf, don't leave..."
His voice Crackles
Like Dry Grass
A Mother can feel her Cub's
Despair
A Mother can also

Reject Her Cub.
In His Eyes I see
His future
Of making His Large Branch Cave
At the Cost of
Moon's Blood
And Defending It
His Stealing of She-Men,
The Way the She-Men
Stop their Packs
From Fighting
By using their Cubs.
All I Know Is
I will Not Be There
When Not-Man
Comes to Take
Sun With Him
I will be with Moon
And We Will
Be Walking
By The River.

I Am She-Wolf

I am She-Wolf of the Forest
I have Told You What Happened
By The River.
I have had Cubs And Revenge
My Mate Has Been Avenged.
Over time, Sun's Pack
Amused Me
By putting up a Stone Version
Of Myself Suckling Sun and Moon
At Not-Man's Urging.
I Look Out for Them
As I did
Sun and Moon.
Sun is with Not-Man
And Moon, Well

Moon is with Me
By the River
As We Always Will Be
And Woodpecker
Is Here Too,
Our Souls
Fly Along the River-Bank
Gathering Speed
Until All I can Do
Is Lift up my Head
And HOWL
I AM SHE-WOLF.

Acknowledgements

I would like to acknowledge Ray Wilkinson and Wendy Turner for their help with editing and typesetting this work. I am grateful to Verulam Writers for their support along the way.

Printed in Great Britain
by Amazon